FLIGHT FROM TOMORROW

FLIGHT FROM TOMORROW

by H. Beam Piper

There was no stopping General Zarvas' rebellion. Hunted and hated in two worlds, Hradzka dreamed of a monomaniac's glory, stranded in the past with his knowledge of the future. But he didn't know the past quite well enough....

1

But yesterday, a whole planet had shouted: *Hail Hradzka! Hail the Leader!* Today, they were screaming:*Death to Hradzka! Kill the tyrant!*

The Palace, where Hradzka, surrounded by his sycophants and guards, had lorded it over a solar system, was now an inferno. Those who had been too closely identified with the dictator's rule to hope for forgiveness were fighting to the last, seeking only a quick death in combat; one by one, their isolated points of resistance were being wiped out. The corridors and chambers of the huge palace were thronged with rebels, loud with their shouts, and with the rasping hiss of heat-beams and the crash of blasters, reeking with the stench of scorched plastic and burned flesh, of hot metal and charred fabric. The living quarters were overrun; the mob smashed down walls and tore up floors in search of secret hiding-places. They found strange things—the space-ship that had been built under one of the domes, in readiness for flight to the still-loyal colonies on Mars or the Asteroid Belt, for instance—but Hradzka himself they could not find.

At last, the search reached the New Tower which reared its head five thousand feet above the palace, the highest thing in the city. They blasted down the huge steel doors, cut the power from the energy-screens. They landed from antigrav-cars on the upper levels. But except for barriers of metal and concrete and energy, they met with no opposition. Finally, they came to the spiral stairway which led up to the great metal sphere which capped the whole structure.

General Zarvas, the Army Commander who had placed himself at the head of the revolt, stood with his foot on the lowest step, his followers behind him. There was Prince Burvanny, the leader of the old nobility, and Ghorzesko Orhm, the merchant, and between them stood Tobbh, the chieftain of the mutinous slaves. There were clerks; laborers; poor but haughty nobles: and wealthy merchants who had long been forced to hide their riches from the dictator's tax-gatherers, and soldiers, and spacemen.

"You'd better let some of us go first sir," General Zarvas' orderly, a blood-stained bandage about his head, his uniform in rags, suggested. "You don't know what might be up there."

The General shook his head. "I'll go first." Zarvas Pol was not the man to send subordinates into danger ahead of himself. "To tell the truth, I'm afraid we won't find anything at all up there."

"You mean...?" Ghorzesko Orhm began.

"The 'time-machine'," Zarvas Pol replied. "If he's managed to get it finished, the Great Mind only knows where he may be, now. Or when."

He loosened the blaster in his holster and started up the long spiral. His followers spread out, below; sharp-shooters took position to cover his ascent. Prince Burvanny and Tobbh the Slave started to follow him. They hesitated as each motioned the other to precede him; then the nobleman followed the general, his blaster drawn, and the brawny slave behind him.

The door at the top was open, and Zarvas Pol stepped through but there was nothing in the great spherical room except a raised dais some fifty feet in diameter, its polished metal top strangely clean and empty. And a crumpled heap of burned cloth and charred flesh that had, not long ago, been a man. An old man with a white beard, and the seven-pointed star of the Learned Brothers on his breast, advanced to meet the armed intruders.

"So he is gone, Kradzy Zago?" Zarvas Pol said, holstering his weapon. "Gone in the 'time-machine', to hide in yesterday or tomorrow. And you let him go?"

The old one nodded. "He had a blaster, and I had none." He indicated the body on the floor. "Zoldy Jarv had no blaster, either, but he tried to stop Hradzka. See, he squandered his life as a fool squanders his money, getting nothing for it. And a man's life is not money, Zarvas Pol."

"I do not blame you, Kradzy Zago," General Zarvas said. "But now you must get to work, and build us another 'time-machine', so that we can hunt him down."

"Does revenge mean so much to you, then?"

The soldier made an impatient gesture. "Revenge is for fools, like that pack of screaming beasts below. I do not kill for revenge; I kill because dead men do no harm."

"Hradzka will do us no more harm," the old scientist replied. "He is a thing of yesterday; of a time long past and half-lost in the mists of legend."

"No matter. As long as he exists, at any point in space-time, Hradzka is still a threat. Revenge means much to Hradzka; he will return for it, when we least expect him."

The old man shook his head. "No, Zarvas Pol, Hradzka will not return."

*

Hradzka holstered his blaster, threw the switch that sealed the "time-machine", put on the antigrav-unit and started the time-shift unit. He reached out and set the destination-dial for the mid-Fifty-Second Century of the Atomic Era. That would land him in the Ninth Age of Chaos, following the Two-Century War and the collapse of the World Theocracy. A good time for his purpose: the world would be slipping back into barbarism, and yet possess the technologies of former civilizations. A hundred little national states would be trying to regain social stability, competing and warring with one another. Hradzka glanced back over his shoulder at the cases of books, record-spools, tri-dimensional pictures, and scale-models. These people of the past would welcome him and his science of the future, would make him their leader.

He would start in a small way, by taking over the local feudal or tribal government, would arm his followers with weapons of the future. Then he would impose his rule upon neighboring tribes, or princedoms, or communes, or whatever, and build a strong sovereignty; from that he envisioned a world empire, a Solar System empire.

Then, he would build "time-machines", many "time-machines". He would recruit an army such as the universe had never seen, a swarm of men from every age in the past. At that point, he would return to the Hundredth Century of the Atomic Era, to wreak vengeance upon those who had risen against him. A slow smile grew on Hradzka's thin lips as he thought of the tortures with which he would put Zarvas Pol to death.

He glanced up at the great disc of the indicator and frowned. Already he was back to the year 7500, A.E., and the temporal-displacement had not begun to slow. The disc was turning even more rapidly—7000, 6000, 5500; he gasped slightly. Then he had passed his destination; he was now in the Fortieth Century, but the indicator was slowing. The hairline crossed the Thirtieth Century, the Twentieth, the Fifteenth, the Tenth. He wondered what had gone wrong, but he had recovered from his fright by this time. When this insane machine stopped, as it must around the First Century of the Atomic Era, he would investigate, make repairs, then shift forward to his target-point. Hradzka was determined upon the Fifty-Second Century; he had made a special study of the history of that period, had learned the language spoken then, and he understood the methods necessary to gain power over the natives of that time.

The indicator-disc came to a stop, in the First Century. He switched on the magnifier and leaned forward to look; he had emerged into normal time in the year 10 of the Atomic Era, a decade after the first uranium-pile had gone into operation, and seven years after the first atomic bombs had been exploded in warfare. The altimeter showed that he was hovering at eight thousand feet above ground-level.

Slowly, he cut out the antigrav, letting the "time machine" down

8

easily. He knew that there had been no danger of materializing inside anything; the New Tower had been built to put it above anything that had occupied that space-point at any moment within history, or legend, or even the geological knowledge of man. What lay below, however, was uncertain. It was night—the visi-screen showed only a star-dusted, moonless-sky, and dark shadows below. He snapped another switch; for a few micro-seconds a beam of intense light was turned on, automatically photographing the landscape under him. A second later, the developed picture was projected upon another screen; it showed only wooded mountains and a barren, brush-grown valley.

*

The "time-machine" came to rest with a soft jar and a crashing of broken bushes that was audible through the sound pickup. Hradzka pulled the main switch; there was a click as the shielding went out and the door opened. A breath of cool night air drew into the hollow sphere.

Then there was a loud *bang* inside the mechanism, and a flash of blue-white light which turned to pinkish flame with a nasty crackling. Curls of smoke began to rise from the square black box that housed the "time-shift" mechanism, and from behind the instrument-board. In a moment, everything was glowing-hot: driblets of aluminum and silver were running down from the instruments. Then the whole interior of the "time-machine" was afire; there was barely time for Hradzka to leap through the open door.

The brush outside impeded him, and he used his blaster to clear a path for himself away from the big sphere, which was now glowing faintly on the outside. The heat grew in intensity, and the brush outside was taking fire. It was not until he had gotten two hundred yards from the machine that he stopped, realizing what had happened.

The machine, of course, had been sabotaged. That would have been young Zoldy, whom he had killed, or that old billy-goat, Kradzy

Zago; the latter, most likely. He cursed both of them for having marooned him in this savage age, at the very beginning of atomic civilization, with all his printed and recorded knowledge destroyed. Oh, he could still gain mastery over these barbarians; he knew enough to fashion a crude blaster, or a heat-beam gun, or an atomic-electric conversion unit. But without his books and records, he could never build an antigrav unit, and the secret of the "temporal shift" was lost.

For "Time" is not an object, or a medium which can be travelled along. The "Time-Machine" was not a vehicle; it was a mechanical process of displacement within the space-time continuum, and those who constructed it knew that it could not be used with the sort of accuracy that the dials indicated. Hradzka had ordered his scientists to produce a "Time Machine", and they had combined the possible—displacement within the space-time continuum—with the sort of fiction the dictator demanded, for their own well-being. Even had there been no sabotage, his return to his own "time" was nearly of zero probability.

The fire, spreading from the "time-machine", was blowing toward him; he observed the wind-direction and hurried around out of the path of the flames. The light enabled him to pick his way through the brush, and, after crossing a small stream, he found a rutted road and followed it up the mountainside until he came to a place where he could rest concealed until morning.

2

It was broad daylight when he woke, and there was a strange throbbing sound; Hradzka lay motionless under the brush where he had slept, his blaster ready. In a few minutes, a vehicle came into sight, following the road down the mountainside.

It was a large thing, four-wheeled, with a projection in front which probably housed the engine and a cab for the operator. The body of the vehicle was simply an open rectangular box. There were two men in the cab, and about twenty or thirty more crowded into the box body. These were dressed in faded and nondescript garments of blue and gray and brown; all were armed with crude weapons—axes, bill-hooks, long-handled instruments with serrated edges, and what looked like broad-bladed spears. The vehicle itself, which seemed to be propelled by some sort of chemical-explosion engine, was dingy and mud-splattered; the men in it were ragged and unshaven. Hradzka snorted in contempt; they were probably warriors of the local tribe, going to the fire in the belief that it had been started by raiding enemies. When they found the wreckage of the "time-machine", they would no doubt believe that it was the chariot of some god and drag it home to be venerated.

A plan of action was taking shape in his mind. First, he must get clothing of the sort worn by these people, and find a safe hiding-place for his own things. Then, pretending to be a deaf-mute, he would go among them to learn something of their customs and pick up the language. When he had done that, he would move on to another tribe or village, able to tell a credible story for himself. For a while, it would be necessary for him to do menial work, but in the end, he would establish himself among these people. Then he could gather around him a faction of those who were dissatisfied with whatever conditions existed, organize a conspiracy, make arms for his followers, and start his program of power-seizure.

The matter of clothing was attended to shortly after he had crossed the mountain and descended into the valley on the other side. Hearing a clinking sound some distance from the road, as of metal striking stone, Hradzka stole cautiously through the woods until he came within sight of a man who was digging with a mattock, uprooting small bushes of a particular sort, with rough gray bark and three-pointed leaves. When he had dug one up, he would cut off the roots and then slice away the root-bark with a knife, putting it into a sack. Hradzka's lip curled contemptuously; the fellow was gathering the stuff for medicinal use. He had heard of the use of roots and herbs for such purposes by the ancient savages.

The blaster would be no use here; it was too powerful, and would destroy the clothing that the man was wearing. He unfastened a strap from his belt and attached it to a stone to form a hand-loop, then, inched forward behind the lone herb-gatherer. When he was close enough, he straightened and rushed forward, swinging his improvised weapon. The man heard him and turned, too late.

*

After undressing his victim, Hradzka used the mattock to finish him, and then to dig a grave. The fugitive buried his own clothes with the murdered man, and donned the faded blue shirt, rough shoes, worn trousers and jacket. The blaster he concealed under the jacket, and he kept a few other Hundredth Century gadgets; these he would hide somewhere closer to his center of operations.

He had kept, among other things, a small box of food-concentrate capsules, and in one pocket of the newly acquired jacket he found a package containing food. It was rough and unappetizing fare—slices of cold cooked meat between slices of some cereal substance. He ate these before filling in the grave, and put the paper wrappings in with the dead man. Then, his work finished, he threw the mattock into the brush and set out again, grimacing disgustedly and scratching himself. The clothing he had appropriated was verminous.

Crossing another mountain, he descended into a second valley, and, for a time, lost his way among a tangle of narrow ravines. It was dark by the time he mounted a hill and found himself looking down another valley, in which a few scattered lights gave evidence of human habitations. Not wishing to arouse suspicion by approaching these in the night-time, he found a place among some young evergreens where he could sleep.

The next morning, having breakfasted on a concentrate capsule, he found a hiding-place for his blaster in a hollow tree. It was in a sufficiently prominent position so that he could easily find it again, and at the same time unlikely to be discovered by some native. Then he went down into the inhabited valley.

He was surprised at the ease with which he established contact with the natives. The first dwelling which he approached, a cluster of farm-buildings at the upper end of the valley, gave him shelter. There was a man, clad in the same sort of rough garments Hradzka had taken from the body of the herb-gatherer, and a woman in a faded and shapeless dress. The man was thin and work-bent; the woman short and heavy. Both were past middle age.

He made inarticulate sounds to attract their attention, then gestured to his mouth and ears to indicate his assumed affliction. He rubbed his stomach to portray hunger. Looking about, he saw an ax sticking in a chopping-block, and a pile of wood near it, probably the fuel used by these people. He took the ax, split up some of the wood, then repeated the hunger-signs. The man and the woman both nodded, laughing; he was shown a pile of tree-limbs, and the man picked up a short billet of wood and used it like a measuring-rule, to indicate that all the wood was to be cut to that length.

Hradzka fell to work, and by mid-morning, he had all the wood cut. He had seen a circular stone, mounted on a trestle with a metal axle through it, and judged it to be some sort of a grinding-wheel, since it was fitted with a foot-pedal and a rusty metal can was set above it to spill water onto the grinding-edge. After chopping the wood, he carefully sharpened the ax, handing it to the man for inspection. This seemed to please the man; he clapped Hradzka on the shoulder, making commendatory sounds.

*

It required considerable time and ingenuity to make himself a more or less permanent member of the household. Hradzka had made a survey of the farmyard, noting the sorts of work that would normally be performed on the farm, and he pantomimed this work in its simpler operations. He pointed to the east, where the sun would rise, and to the zenith, and to the west. He made signs indicative of eating, and of sleeping, and of rising, and of working. At length, he succeeded in conveying his meaning.

There was considerable argument between the man and the woman, but his proposal was accepted, as he expected that it would. It was easy to see that the work of the farm was hard for this aging couple; now, for a place to sleep and a little food, they were able to acquire a strong and intelligent slave.

In the days that followed, he made himself useful to the farm people; he fed the chickens and the livestock, milked the cow, worked in the fields. He slept in a small room at the top of the house, under the eaves, and ate with the man and woman in the farmhouse kitchen.

It was not long before he picked up a few words which he had heard his employers using, and related them to the things or acts spoken of. And he began to notice that these people, in spite of the crudities of their own life, enjoyed some of the advantages of a fairly complex civilization. Their implements were not hand-craft products, but showed machine workmanship. There were two objects hanging on hooks on the kitchen wall which he was sure were weapons. Both had wooden shoulder-stocks, and wooden fore-pieces; they had long tubes extending to the front, and triggers like blasters. One had double tubes mounted side-by-side, and double triggers; the other had an octagonal tube mounted over a round tube, and a loop extension on the trigger-guard. Then, there was a box on the kitchen wall, with a mouthpiece and a cylindrical tube on a cord. Sometimes a bell would ring out of the box, and the woman would go to this instrument, take down the tube and hold it to her ear, and talk into the mouthpiece. There was another box from which voices would issue, of people conversing, or of orators, or of singing, and sometimes instrumental music. None of these were objects made by savages; these people probably traded with some fairly high civilization. They were not illiterate; he found printed matter, indicating the use of some phonetic alphabet, and paper pamphlets containing printed reproductions of photographs as well as verbal text.

There was also a vehicle on the farm, powered, like the one he had seen on the road, by an engine in which a hydrocarbon liquid-fuel was exploded. He made it his business to examine this minutely, and to study its construction and operation until he was thoroughly familiar with it.

It was not until the third day after his arrival that the chickens began to die. In the morning, Hradzka found three of them dead when he went to feed them, the rest drooping unhealthily; he summoned the man and showed him what he had found. The next morning, they were all dead, and the cow was sick. She gave bloody milk, that evening, and the next morning she lay in her stall and would not get up.

The man and the woman were also beginning to sicken, though both of them tried to continue their work. It was the woman who first noticed that the plants around the farmhouse were withering and turning yellow.

*

The farmer went to the stable with Hradzka and looked at the cow. Shaking his head, he limped back to the house, and returned carrying one of the weapons from the kitchen—the one with the single trigger and the octagonal tube. As he entered the stable, he jerked down and up on the loop extension of the trigger-guard, then put the weapon to his shoulder and pointed it at the cow. It made a flash, and roared louder even than a hand-blaster, and the cow jerked convulsively and was dead. The man then indicated by signs that Hradzka was to drag the dead cow out of the stable, dig a hole, and bury it. This Hradzka did, carefully examining the wound in the cow's head—the weapon, he decided, was not an energy-weapon, but a simple solid-missile projector.

By evening, neither the man nor the woman were able to eat, and both seemed to be suffering intensely. The man used the communicating-instrument on the wall, probably calling on his friends for help. Hradzka did what he could to make them comfortable, cooked his own meal, washed the dishes as he had seen the woman doing, and tidied up the kitchen.

It was not long before people, men and women whom he had seen on the road or who had stopped at the farmhouse while he had been there, began arriving, some carrying baskets of food; and shortly after Hradzka had eaten, a vehicle like the farmer's, but in better condition and of better quality, arrived and a young man got out of it and entered the house, carrying a leather bag. He was apparently some sort of a scientist; he examined the man and his wife, asked many questions, and administered drugs. He also took samples for blood-tests and urinalysis. This, Hradzka considered, was another of the many contradictions he had encountered among these people—this man behaved like an educated scientist, and seemingly had nothing in common with the peasant herb-gatherer on the mountainside.

The fact was that Hradzka was worried. The strange death of the animals, the blight which had smitten the trees and vegetables around the farm, and the sickness of the farmer and his woman, all mystified him. He did not know of any disease which would affect plants and animals and humans; he wondered if some poisonous gas might not be escaping from the earth near the farmhouse. However, he had not, himself, been affected. He also disliked the way in which the doctor and the neighbors seemed to be talking about him. While he had come to a considerable revision of his original opinion about the culture-level of these people, it was not impossible that they might suspect him of having caused the whole thing by witchcraft; at any moment, they might fall upon him and put him to death. In any case, there was no longer any use in his staying here, and it might be wise if he left at once.

Accordingly, he filled his pockets with food from the pantry and slipped out of the farmhouse; before his absence was discovered he was well on his way down the road.

3

That night, Hradzka slept under a bridge across a fairly wide stream; the next morning, he followed the road until he came to a town. It was not a large place; there were perhaps four or five hundred houses and other buildings in it. Most of these were dwellings like the farmhouse where he had been staying, but some were much larger, and seemed to be places of business. One of these latter was a concrete structure with wide doors at the front; inside, he could see men working on the internal-combustion vehicles which seemed to be in almost universal use. Hradzka decided to obtain employment here.

It would be best, he decided, to continue his pretense of being a deaf-mute. He did not know whether a world-language were in use at this time or not, and even if not, the pretense of being a foreigner unable to speak the local dialect might be dangerous. So he entered the vehicle-repair shop and accosted a man in a clean shirt who seemed to be issuing instructions to the workers, going into his pantomime of the homeless mute seeking employment.

The master of the repair-shop merely laughed at him, however. Hradzka became more insistent in his manner, making signs to indicate his hunger and willingness to work. The other men in the shop left their tasks and gathered around; there was much laughter and unmistakably ribald and derogatory remarks. Hradzka was beginning to give up hope of getting employment here when one of the workmen approached the master and whispered something to him.

The two of them walked away, conversing in low voices. Hradzka thought he understood the situation; no doubt the workman, thinking to lighten his own labor, was urging that the vagrant be employed, for no other pay than food and lodging. At length, the master assented to his employee's urgings; he returned, showed Hradzka a hose and a bucket and sponges and cloths, and set him to work cleaning the mud from one of the vehicles. Then, after seeing that the work was being done properly, he went away, entering a room at one side of the shop.

About twenty minutes later, another man entered the shop. He was not dressed like any of the other people whom Hradzka had seen; he wore a gray tunic and breeches, polished black boots, and a cap with a visor and a metal insignia on it; on a belt, he carried a holstered weapon like a blaster.

After speaking to one of the workers, who pointed Hradzka out to him, he approached the fugitive and said something. Hradzka made gestures at his mouth and ears and made gargling sounds; the newcomer shrugged and motioned him to come with him, at the same time producing a pair of handcuffs from his belt and jingling them suggestively.

In a few seconds, Hradzka tried to analyze the situation and estimate its possibilities. The newcomer was a soldier, or, more likely, a policeman, since manacles were a part of his equipment. Evidently, since the evening before, a warning had been made public by means of communicating devices such as he had seen at the farm, advising people that a man of his description, pretending to be a deaf-mute, should be detained and the police notified; it had been for that reason that the workman had persuaded his master to employ Hradzka. No doubt he would be accused of causing the conditions at the farm by sorcery.

*

Hradzka shrugged and nodded, then went to the water-tap to turn off the hose he had been using. He disconnected it, coiled it and hung it up, and then picked up the water-bucket. Then, without warning, he hurled the water into the policeman's face, sprang forward, swinging the bucket by the bale, and hit the man on the head. Releasing his grip on the bucket, he tore the blaster or whatever it was from the holster.

One of the workers swung a hammer, as though to throw it. Hradzka aimed the weapon at him and pulled the trigger; the thing belched fire and kicked back painfully in his hand, and the man fell. He used it again to drop the policeman, then thrust it into the waistband of his trousers and ran outside. The thing was not a blaster at all, he realized—only a missile-projector like the big weapons at the farm, utilizing the force of some chemical explosive.

The policeman's vehicle was standing outside. It was a small, single-seat, two wheeled affair. Having become familiar with the principles of these hydro-carbon engines from examination of the vehicle of the farm, and accustomed as he was to far more complex mechanisms than this crude affair, Hradzka could see at a glance how to operate it. Springing onto the saddle, he kicked away the folding support and started the engine. Just as he did, the master of the repair-shop ran outside, one of the small hand-weapons in his hand, and fired several shots. They all missed, but Hradzka heard the whining sound of the missiles passing uncomfortably close to him.

It was imperative that he recover the blaster he had hidden in the hollow tree at the head of the valley. By this time, there would be a concerted search under way for him, and he needed a better weapon than the solid-missile projector he had taken from the policeman. He did not know how many shots the thing contained, but if it propelled solid missiles by chemical explosion, there could not have been more than five or six such charges in the cylindrical part of the weapon which he had assumed to be the charge-holder. On the other hand, his blaster, a weapon of much greater power, contained enough energy for five hundred blasts, and with it were eight extra energy-capsules, giving him a total of four thousand five hundred blasts.

Handling the two-wheeled vehicle was no particular problem; although he had never ridden on anything of the sort before, it was child's play compared to controlling a Hundredth Century strato-rocket, and Hradzka was a skilled rocket-pilot.

Several times he passed vehicles on the road—the passenger vehicles with enclosed cabins, and cargo-vehicles piled high with farm produce. Once he encountered a large number of children, gathered in front of a big red building with a flagstaff in front, from which a queer flag, with horizontal red and white stripes and a white-spotted blue device in the corner, flew. They scattered off the road in terror at his approach; fortunately, he hit none of them, for at the speed at which he was traveling, such a collision would have wrecked his light vehicle.

*

As he approached the farm where he had spent the past few days, he saw two passenger-vehicles standing by the road. One was a black one, similar to the one in which the physician had come to the farm, and the other was white with black trimmings and bore the same device he had seen on the cap of the policeman. A policeman was sitting in the driver's seat of this vehicle, and another policeman was standing beside it, breathing smoke with one of the white paper cylinders these people used. In the farm-yard, two men were going about with a square black box; to this box, a tube was connected by a wire, and they were passing the tube about over the ground.

The policeman who was standing beside the vehicle saw him approach, and blew his whistle, then drew the weapon from his belt. Hradzka, who had been expecting some attempt to halt him, had let go the right-hand steering handle and drawn his own weapon; as the policeman drew, he fired at him. Without observing the effect of the shot, he sped on; before he had rounded the bend above the farm, several shots were fired after him.

A mile beyond, he came to the place where he had hidden the blaster. He stopped the vehicle and jumped off, plunging into the brush and racing toward the hollow tree. Just as he reached it, he heard a vehicle approach and stop, and the door of the police vehicle slam. Hradzka's fingers found the belt of his blaster; he dragged it out and buckled it on, tossing away the missile weapon he had been carrying.

Then, crouching behind the tree, he waited. A few moments later, he caught a movement in the brush toward the road. He brought up

20

the blaster, aimed and squeezed the trigger. There was a faint bluish glow at the muzzle, and a blast of energy tore through the brush, smashing the molecular structure of everything that stood in the way. There was an involuntary shout of alarm from the direction of the road; at least one of the policemen had escaped the blast. Hradzka holstered his weapon and crept away for some distance, keeping under cover, then turned and waited for some sign of the presence of his enemies. For some time nothing happened; he decided to turn hunter against the men who were hunting him. He started back in the direction of the road, making a wide circle, flitting silently from rock to bush and from bush to tree, stopping often to look and listen.

This finally brought him upon one of the policemen, and almost terminated his flight at the same time. He must have grown over-confident and careless; suddenly a weapon roared, and a missile smashed through the brush inches from his face. The shot had come from his left and a little to the rear. Whirling, he blasted four times, in rapid succession, then turned and fled for a few yards, dropping and crawling behind a rock. When he looked back, he could see wisps of smoke rising from the shattered trees and bushes which had absorbed the energy-output of his weapon, and he caught a faint odor of burned flesh. One of his pursuers, at least, would pursue him no longer.

He slipped away, down into the tangle of ravines and hollows in which he had wandered the day before his arrival at the farm. For the time being, he felt safe, and finally confident that he was not being pursued, he stopped to rest. The place where he stopped seemed familiar, and he looked about. In a moment, he recognized the little stream, the pool where he had bathed his feet, the clump of seedling pines under which he had slept. He even found the silver-foil wrapping from the food concentrate capsule.

But there had been a change, since the night when he had slept here. Then the young pines had been green and alive; now they were blighted, and their needles had turned brown. Hradzka stood for a long time, looking at them. It was the same blight that had touched the plants around the farmhouse. And here, among the pine needles on the ground, lay a dead bird.

It took some time for him to admit, to himself, the implications of vegetation, the chickens, the cow, the farmer and his wife, had all sickened and died. He had been in this place, and now, when he had returned, he found that death had followed him here, too.

*

During the early centuries of the Atomic Era, he knew, there had been great wars, the stories of which had survived even to the Hundredth Century. Among the weapons that had been used, there had been artificial plagues and epidemics, caused by new types of bacteria developed in laboratories, against which the victims had possessed no protection. Those germs and viruses had persisted for centuries, and gradually had lost their power to harm mankind. Suppose, now, that he had brought some of them back with him, to a century before they had been developed. Suppose, that was, that he were a human plague-carrier. He thought of the vermin that had infested the clothing he had taken from the man he had killed on the other side of the mountain; they had not troubled him after the first day.

There was a throbbing mechanical sound somewhere in the air; he looked about, and finally identified its source. A small aircraft had come over the valley from the other side of the mountain and was circling lazily overhead. He froze, shrinking back under a pine-tree; as long as he remained motionless, he would not be seen, and soon the thing would go away. He was beginning to understand why the search for him was being pressed so relentlessly; as long as he remained alive, he was a menace to everybody in this First Century world.

He got out his supply of food concentrates, saw that he had only three capsules left, and put them away again. For a long time, he sat under the dying tree, chewing on a twig and thinking. There must be some way in which he could overcome, or even utilize, his inherent deadliness to these people. He might find some isolated community, conceal himself near it, invade it at night and infect it, and then, when everybody was dead, move in and take it for himself. But was there any such isolated community? The farmhouse where he had worked had been fairly remote, yet its inhabitants had been in communication with the outside world, and the physician had come immediately in response to their call for help.

The little aircraft had been circling overhead, directly above the place where he lay hidden. For a while, Hradzka was afraid it had spotted him, and was debating the advisability of using his blaster on it. Then it banked, turned and went away. He watched it circle over the valley on the other side of the mountain, and got to his feet.

4

Almost at once, there was a new sound—a multiple throbbing, at a quick, snarling tempo that hinted at enormous power, growing louder each second. Hradzka stiffened and drew his blaster; as he did, five more aircraft swooped over the crest of the mountain and came rushing down toward him; not aimlessly, but as though they knew exactly where he was. As they approached, the leading edges of their wings sparkled with light, branches began flying from the trees about him, and there was a loud hammering noise.

He aimed a little in front of them and began blasting. A wing flew from one of the aircraft, and it plunged downward. Another came apart in the air; a third burst into flames. The other two zoomed upward quickly. Hradzka swung his blaster after them, blasting again and again. He hit a fourth with a blast of energy, knocking it to pieces, and then the fifth was out of range. He blasted at it twice, but without effect; a hand-blaster was only good for a thousand yards at the most.

Holstering his weapon, he hurried away, following the stream and keeping under cover of trees. The last of the attacking aircraft had gone away, but the little scout-plane was still circling about, well out of blaster-range.

Once or twice, Hradzka was compelled to stay hidden for some time, not knowing the nature of the pilot's ability to detect him. It was during one of these waits that the next phase of the attack developed.

It began, like the last one, with a distant roar that swelled in volume until it seemed to fill the whole world. Then, fifteen or twenty thousand feet out of blaster-range, the new attackers swept into sight.

There must have been fifty of them, huge tapering things with wide-spread wings, flying in close formation, wave after V-shaped wave. He stood and stared at them, amazed; he had never imagined that such aircraft existed in the First Century. Then a high-pitched screaming sound cut through the roar of the propellers, and for an instant he saw countless small specks in the sky, falling downward.

The first bomb-salvo landed in the young pines, where he had fought against the first air attack. Great gouts of flame shot upward, and smoke, and flying earth and debris. Hradzka turned and started to run. Another salvo fell in front of him; he veered to the left and plunged on through the undergrowth. Now the bombs were falling all about him, deafening him with their thunder, shaking him with concussion. He dodged, frightened, as the trunk of a tree came crashing down beside him. Then something hit him across the back, knocking him flat. For a moment, he lay stunned, then tried to rise. As he did, a searing light filled his eyes and a wave of intolerable heat swept over him. Then darkness....

*

"No, Zarvas Pol," Kradzy Zago repeated. "Hradzka will not return; the 'time-machine' was sabotaged."

"So? By you?" the soldier asked.

The scientist nodded. "I knew the purpose for which he intended it. Hradzka was not content with having enslaved a whole Solar

System: he hungered to bring tyranny and serfdom to all the past and all the future as well; he wanted to be master not only of the present but of the centuries that were and were to be, as well. I never took part in politics, Zarvas Pol; I had no hand in this revolt. But I could not be party to such a crime as Hradzka contemplated when it lay within my power to prevent it."

"The machine will take him out of our space-time continuum, or back to a time when this planet was a swirling cloud of flaming gas?" Zarvas Pol asked.

Kradzy Zago shook his head. "No, the unit is not powerful enough for that. It will only take him about ten thousand years into the past. But then, when it stops, the machine will destroy itself. It may destroy Hradzka with it or he may escape. But if he does, he will be left stranded ten thousand years ago, when he can do us no harm.

"Actually, it did not operate as he imagined and there is an infinitely small chance that he could have returned to our 'time', in any event. But I wanted to insure against even so small a chance."

"We can't be sure of that," Zarvas Pol objected. "He may know more about the machine than you think; enough more to build another like it. So you must build me a machine and I'll take back a party of volunteers and hunt him down."

"That would not be necessary, and you would only share his fate." Then, apparently changing the subject, Kradzy Zago asked: "Tell me, Zarvas Pol; have you never heard the legends of the Deadly Radiations?"

General Zarvas smiled. "Who has not? Every cadet at the Officers' College dreams of re-discovering them, to use as a weapon, but nobody ever has. We hear these tales of how, in the early days, atomic engines and piles and fission-bombs emitted particles which were utterly deadly, which would make anything with which they came in contact deadly, which would bring a horrible death to any human being. But these are only myths. All the ancient experiments have been duplicated time and again, and the deadly radiation effect

25

has never been observed. Some say that it is a mere old-wives' terror tale; some say that the deaths were caused by fear of atomic energy, when it was still unfamiliar; others contend that the fundamental nature of atomic energy has altered by the degeneration of the fissionable matter. For my own part, I'm not enough of a scientist to have an opinion."

*

The old one smiled wanly. "None of these theories are correct. In the beginning of the Atomic Era, the Deadly Radiations existed. They still exist, but they are no longer deadly, because all life on this planet has adapted itself to such radiations, and all living things are now immune to them."

"And Hradzka has returned to a time when such immunity did not exist? But would that not be to his advantage?"

"Remember, General, that man has been using atomic energy for ten thousand years. Our whole world has become drenched with radioactivity. The planet, the seas, the atmosphere, and every living thing, are all radioactive, now. Radioactivity is as natural to us as the air we breathe. Now, you remember hearing of the great wars of the first centuries of the Atomic Era, in which whole nations were wiped out, leaving only hundreds of survivors out of millions. You, no doubt, think that such tales are products of ignorant and barbaric imagination, but I assure you, they are literally true. It was not the blast-effect of a few bombs which created such holocausts, but the radiations released by the bombs. And those who survived to carry on the race were men and women whose systems resisted the radiations, and they transmitted to their progeny that power of resistance. In many cases, their children were mutants—not monsters, although there were many of them, too, which did not survive—but humans who were immune to radioactivity."

"An interesting theory, Kradzy Zago," the soldier commented. "And one which conforms both to what we know of atomic energy and to the ancient legends. Then you would say that those radiations

26

are still deadly—to the non-immune?"

"Exactly. And Hradzka, his body emitting those radiations, has returned to the First Century of the Atomic Era—to a world without immunity."

General Zarvas' smile vanished. "Man!" he cried in horror. "You have loosed a carrier of death among those innocent people of the past!"

Kradzy Zago nodded. "That is true. I estimate that Hradzka will probably cause the death of a hundred or so people, before he is dealt with. But dealt with he will be. Tell me, General; if a man should appear now, out of nowhere, spreading a strange and horrible plague wherever he went, what would you do?"

"Why, I'd hunt him down and kill him," General Zarvas replied. "Not for anything he did, but for the menace he was. And then, I'd cover his body with a mass of concrete bigger than this palace."

"Precisely." Kradzy Zago smiled. "And the military commanders and political leaders of the First Century were no less ruthless or efficient than you. You know how atomic energy was first used? There was an ancient nation, upon the ruins of whose cities we have built our own, which was famed for its idealistic humanitarianism. Yet that nation, treacherously attacked, created the first atomic bombs in self defense, and used them. It is among the people of that nation that Hradzka has emerged."

"But would they recognize him as the cause of the calamity he brings among them?"

"Of course. He will emerge at the time when atomic energy is first being used. They will have detectors for the Deadly Radiations—detectors we know nothing of, today, for a detection instrument must be free from the thing it is intended to detect, and today everything is radioactive. It will be a day or so before they discover what is happening to them, and not a few will die in that time, I fear; but once they have found out what is killing their people, Hradzka's days—no, his hours—will be numbered."

FLIGHT FROM TOMORROW

"A mass of concrete bigger than this place," Tobbh the Slave repeated General Zarvas' words. "*The Ancient Spaceport!*"

Prince Burvanny clapped him on the shoulder. "Tobbh, man! You've hit it!"

"You mean...?" Kradzy Zago began.

"Yes. You all know of it. It's stood for nobody knows how many millennia, and nobody's ever decided what it was, to begin with, except that somebody, once, filled a valley with concrete, level from mountain-top to mountain-top. The accepted theory is that it was done for a firing-stand for the first Moon-rocket. But gentlemen, our friend Tobbh's explained it. It is the tomb of Hradzka, and it has been the tomb of Hradzka for ten thousand years before Hradzka was born!"